SPACE TRAVELLERS

For Nard and Nellie. GR

Originally published in Australia in 1992 by Ashton Scholastic Pty. Limited.

Text copyright © 1992 by Margaret Wild.
Illustrations copyright © 1992 by Gregory Rogers.
All rights reserved. Published by Scholastic Inc.,
730 Broadway, New York, NY 10003, by arrangement with
Ashton Scholastic Pty. Limited.
SCHOLASTIC HARDCOVER is a registered trademark of Scholastic Inc.

Library of Congress Cataloging-in-Publication Data

Wild, Margaret, 1948 –
    Space travellers / by Margaret Wild; illustrated by Greg Rogers.
        p.   cm.
    Summary: Homeless in the big city, Zac and his mother live in a
rocket in the middle of a park until they can find a real home.
    ISBN 0-590-45598-2
    [1. Homeless persons — Fiction.] I. Rogers, Greg, ill.
II. Title.
PZ7.W64574Sp 1992
[E] — dc20   91-32052
                                                         CIP
                                                         AC

12 11 10 9 8 7 6 5 4 3 2 1   3 4 5 6 7 8/9

Printed in U.S.A.   44

First Scholastic printing, April 1993

SPACE TRAVELLERS

by Margaret Wild

Illustrated by
Gregory Rogers

SCHOLASTIC INC.
NEW YORK

Lately, Zac and his mother, Mandy,
have been sleeping in a rocket.

Every evening, at sunset, Zac and
Mandy climb up into the rocket, unroll
their sleeping bags, and switch on the torch.
Mandy pours the milk and slices the
cheese, while Zac butters the bread.

Then Mandy plays the flute and Zac listens,
eyes closed. In the distance, dogs bark and
sirens scream, but Zac is sure he can feel the
rocket zooming through the clouds,
past the moon, up towards the stars.

"We're lucky to sleep in a rocket," says Zac, and Mandy tries to smile. She's all scrunched up and her neck aches and the nights are getting colder.

But it is true, they are lucky to have found the rocket. Much luckier than their friends, Simon and Ron and Dorothy.

"Dorothy likes our rocket," says Zac. "If it were bigger, she could sleep in it, too. Then she could bring her cat."

"She doesn't have a cat," yawns Mandy.

"Not yet," says Zac, "but if she slept in a rocket, she could have one."

Mandy sighs. "Time to go to sleep," she says. Zac switches off the torch...

. . . and all is dark and quiet
in outer, outer space.

The weeks go by, and Zac and Mandy are
still sleeping in the rocket. One Monday
morning they roll up their sleeping bags,
as usual, brush the crumbs out of the rocket,
and go to the rest rooms at the railway station.

Zac washes his face and brushes his teeth with his finger. Mandy washes her hair in the basin and blows it dry under the hand-dryer.

She checks Zac out. "Not bad, mate, even though you've got potatoes growing behind your ears. Tomorrow night you're going to have a proper bath."

"A proper bath?" says Zac. "Where?"

Mandy twirls him round and round. "Surprise!" she yells. "D'ya remember Lil and Rick? They've managed to get an old house in the city, and we can stay with them for a while. Just think! A room of our own!"

Zac feels dizzy. A room of their own? A room
with a bed and a bath, perhaps even a TV?
But what about the rocket? What about the
moon and the stars and all those planets,
still to be explored, in outer, outer space?

Mandy touches his cheek. "We can't stay
in the rocket forever, you know. Now we've
got somewhere decent to live, I can try to
get a job, and you can start school. Okay?"

"Okay," says Zac, and it *is* okay, really. But
he feels as though he has lost something,
and he is very quiet when they join Ron and
Simon and Dorothy for breakfast.

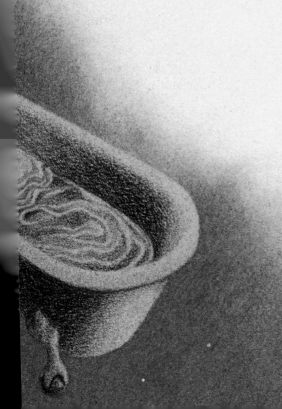

It is a feast. Simon has some hot dogs
the butcher gave him. Ron has six
bread rolls. Dorothy has a flask of tea from
the hairdresser on the corner, and Zac and
Mandy hand around the last of their cheese.

"So tell us, space travellers," says Simon,
"where did ya go last night? Jupiter or Mars?"

"Pluto, actually," says Zac.

"Pluto, actually," echoes Dorothy.
"Fancy that!"
"It's smaller than the moon and very cold,"
says Zac. "Just as well Mom and I were
wearing our jackets."

"Fancy that!" says Dorothy, and Zac can
tell she very, very much wants to be a
space traveller, too.
Dorothy and the-cat-she-doesn't-yet-have.

"Listen, folks," says Mandy quietly. "We're moving into a room tomorrow. Here's the address, and when it's cold and raining we'll squeeze you all in, too, somehow. Okay?"

"Okay," nod Simon and Ron, but Dorothy says suddenly, "What about the rocket?"

Mandy grins and rubs her neck. "The rocket is yours, Dorothy, if you want it. But, I warn you, it's not very comfortable."

"Mine?" says Dorothy. "Mine!" And the sun is in her smile, and a million billion stars in her eyes.

"You'll get space-sick, woman," jokes Ron.
"Bet you don't get further than the moon,"
says Simon, smiling at Zac.

But Dorothy just gives them all another
wide, dazed smile, and hobbles off quick
smart to the library to find out everything
about Jupiter and Mars and Pluto, actually.

That night, the very last night
in the rocket, Zac and Mandy
decide to travel far and fast.

"Shut your eyes tight,"
says Mandy. "As tight as tight
can be. Ready? Blast off!"

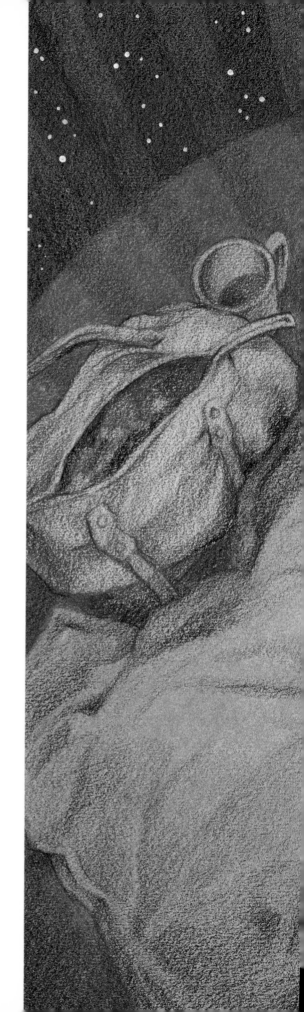

In the morning, Dorothy is waiting
on the bottom step.
Dorothy and the-cat-she-now-has.

Zac shows her around the rocket and tells
her about moonquakes and shooting stars
and comets. "There's even an enormous
black hole," he says, "right in the middle
of the galaxy."

"Fancy that!" says Dorothy, and Zac can
tell she is just itching for it to be night.

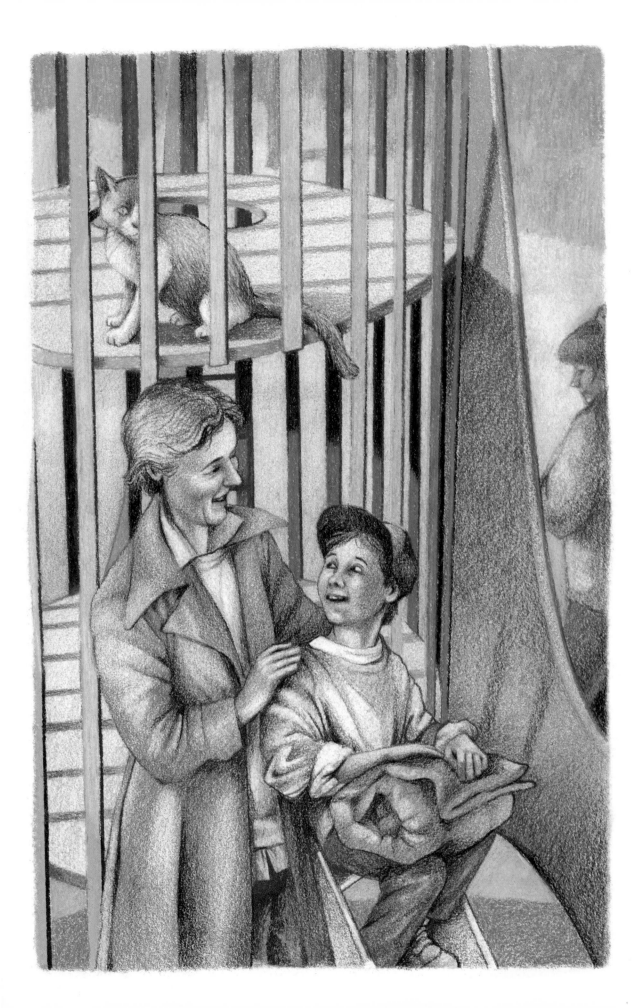

Zac and Mandy wave good-bye until they can't see Dorothy any more.

"She'll make a good space traveller," says Zac, and he and Mandy each take a deep breath and march quick smart towards their new room in the city.